Title: *Super - Over*

Author: John F King

Publisher: York Europe

ISBN: 978-1-8383426-0-9

# Super - Over

By

John F King

York Europe Publications

2021

©

www.johnkinginternational.co.uk

# *Super - Over*

## Batting order-

Over

Sight Test


Close of Play

Picked

Six


World keeps spinning

The real thing


I C C


-

# Over

*A new audio play/Super Over/Drama King II*

2021

**1 EXT ACOUSTIC – DAYTIME**

FX **THE ROAR OF A SPORTS CROWD AT MAJOR OCCASION**

**COMMENTATOR** OVER THE CROWD

…This day of history, whatever happens, this day people will talk about for decades to come…

THE SOUND CHANGES TO INT ACOUSTIC -IT IS A RECORDING OF THE BROADCAST HEARD ON SOUND BAR INSIDE A ROOM

A TELEPHONE IS RINGING INCESSANTLY.

THE SOUNDS MIX AND BUILD CLEARLY HEARD BY **EILEEN VANE** IN ADJACENT ROOM

EILEEN

Please God, make it stop or…

SHE OPENS THE DOOR INTO THE NEXT ROOM WHERE THE SOUNDS ORIGINATE, WITHIN THE WALL OF SOUND SHE IS TRYING TO FIND THE CONTROL. THE ROOM IS SMOKE-FILLED, FULL OF EMPTY BOTTLES, CANS, TAKE AWAY PACKAGES, OLD NEWSPAPERS…

EILEEN

Smoke everywhere, can't see, can't think. Where is the control?

SHE FINDS IT AND MUTES THE TV SYSTEM.

HERBERT 'CARLY' **VANE**

I was watching that.

EILEEN

Answer the phone. Take it.

SHE LIFTS THE PHONE AND HANDS IT TO HERBERT.

VANE INTO PHONE

Wrong number.

**VOICE** ( **PERCIVAL SAMUELS 'P S'** ) ON TELEPHONE

Mr Herbert Vane?

VANE

Wrong number

VOICE ( P S ) ON TELEPHONE

Herbert, if I may, Herb?

VANE

How did you get this number?

VOICE ( P S ) ON TELEPHONE

So it is the right number?

VANE

You people, putting words in my mouth.

HE SLAMS TELEPHONE RECEIVER DOWN SO HARD IT BOUNCES UP AND THE RING TONE CAN BE HEARD.

EILEEN

Who was that on the telephone? Who was it? Answer. Herbert.

STAND OFF

EILEEN

State of this room. State of you.

SHE PICKS UP TELEPHONE AND REPLACES IT.

VANE

Give me the remote. I was watching television. Give it to me.

STAND OFF

EILEEN GIVES IT TO HIM, EXITS SLAMMING DOOR. BRIEF SILENCE. HE FLICKS TV ON AGAIN, ROAR OF SPORTS CROWD RESUMES

COMMENTATOR ON TV SPEAKING OVER THE CROWD

…that is the equation, 9 runs required, two balls remaining. It's Brian Baptiste – known, inevitably as John – on strike. No I am not going to use a biblical analogy, it isn't about faith, it's about belief. Can these two do it? The bowler is at his mark, turning now, in, beautiful delivery, Baptiste drives, contact good but is it good enough? It's pulled up inside the boundary, they will have to run them down, two, three. So this is what it all comes down to. Herbert Vane on strike, one delivery remaining, 6 required to win.

No, I am not going to talk about destiny, it's only a game. The bowler is running in, Herbert Vane hits.

The ball is high in the air…

EILEEN HAS RE-ENTERED AND SHARPLY SWITCHES TV OFF. SILENCE.

HERBERT VANE LIGHTS CIGARETTE AND OPENS BOTTLE.

VANE

Do I have to repeat myself? I was watching that.

EILEEN

You, we, everyone has seen it before. Many times. A long time
ago.

Watch something new. Please. Change the channel. VANE IS
SMOKING, SWIGGING FROM BOTTLE. Open the window, let some fresh
air in.

VANE

Switch it on. I am not asking again.

EILEEN

It's rude to have the TV on when you have visitors.

VANE

Tell them I don't want to see anyone.

EILEEN     (LEAVING)

Can't breathe in here.

VANE        (SHOUTING)

Tell them I'm not in.

EILEEN (ON WAY OUT)

He's in there, John. As usual.

**BRIAN 'JOHN' BAPTISTE**

(TO EILEEN) Thanks, love. (ENTERING, TO VANE) Not too bright
that, man, shouting out I'm not in. Losing your touch? Jeez,
stink of this...room.

VANE

What do you want, Baptiste?

BAPTISTE

Nice to see you, Herbert.

VANE

Shut up, close the door.

BAPTISTE

Look, Herb, mate, this is no way to live. I've an idea, a way out, for you. I've talked to some people about

VANE

I said close the door, behind you.

VANE FLICKS TV BACK ON AGAIN

COMMENTATOR ON THE TV ABOVE A CHEERING CROWD

… I have not seen anything like this before, I'm not sure I ever will again…

BAPTISTE STRUGGLING AGAINST THE SOUND OF THE TV

…A way back, listen…

THE TV AT HIGH VOLUME

BAPTISTE LEAVES THE ROOM, TV CAN STILL BE HEARD THROUGH THE DOOR

EILEEN

I appreciate you coming, John.

BAPTISTE

How is he, Eileen? Actually,you know what, how are you, how are you holding up, love?

EILEEN

Do you want to tell me your idea, John, sorry Brian these days.

BAPTISTE

I'll come back another time, when the TV is off.

EILEEN

That time will never come. I know you are being loyal. I appreciate you coming.

BAPTISTE

Got to go now. You know how it is, Eileen love, night before a game.

EXTERNAL DOOR CLOSES AS BRIAN LEAVES, EILEEN REMAINS INSIDE, BLARE OF TV AUDIBLE THROUGH DOORS. FADE DOWN

**INT ACOUSTIC — EVENING**

FADE UP FX **THEATRE PA** ANNOUNCEMENT

Ladies and gentlemen, there will now be an interval.

This evenings performance of *Noises Off* will recommence in 20 minutes...

EILEEN

John. What are you doing here?

BAPTISTE

Nice to see you too , Eileen.

**OCEAN**

You are a rude woman, whatever your name is.

EILEEN

I'm sorry all. This is Daljit.

**DALJIT DASS**

Good evening everyone.

BAPTISTE

Hey Daljit. This is my fiancée, Ocean. Ocean, Daljit, Eileen.

OCEAN

You know I don't mean the introductions, Brian. It is the statement, the implication that you shouldn't be at the theatre.

EILEEN

I'm sorry. You know that isn't what I meant

DALJIT

Ladies, ladies

EILEEN

Sorry...

OCEAN

Don't keep saying sorry. You are rude and repetitive. How tedious. Brian, I assume you pre-ordered a drink. I want a drink now.

THEATRE P A

This evenings performance will recommence in 15 minutes. A full range of alcoholic and soft drinks, tea, coffee…

DALJIT

I'll help Brian carry the drinks

THEATRE P A

…light refreshments are available

OCEAN MOVING BRIAN AWAY

Move it Brian, they can fetch their own drinks

BRIAN

But…

THEY MOVE AWAY IN CROWDED INTERVAL BAR

DALJIT TO EILEEN

Come on Eileen. There is an atmosphere. I think we should go over to them. Ocean doesn't seem the type to make the first move.

EILEEN

You go if you must, Daljit darling. No one speaks to me like that.

DALJIT

Don't they?

DALJIT MOVES ACROSS THE ROOM. ABOVE THE CROWD OCEAN IS SPEAKING TO BRIAN BAPTISTE

OCEAN

What is it with these nicknames? Carly, Darling, calling my Brian John ?

BRIAN

County circuit. Kind of happens Inevitably, in-crowd.

OCEAN

Nothing is inevitable, Brian. Why do you need in-crowds?

DALJIT JOINING THEM

I thought I would cross the room. Offer my congratulations. Your engagement.

THEATRE P A

This evenings performance of *Noises Off* will recommence shortly, please…

OCEAN   BEAT

Daljit isn't it? That is kind, isn't it Brian. Ask Eileen to come over.

BRIAN

Yes, darling. Let me get Daljit and Eileen a…

THEATRE P A

Retake your seats

OCEAN

Timing, Brian. There is - was - an atmosphere. We should all get together after the show and reframe.

DALJIT

A reframe would be most congenial.


3

**EXT / INT THE SAME EVENING - LATER**

CLICK OF DOOR HANDLE AS EILEEN, DALJIT, OCEAN AND BAPTISTE RETURN FROM THEATRE TO EILEEN AND HERBERT VANE'S HOUSE. THE MUFFLED SOUND HERBERT'S CRICKET LOOP ON THE TV IS HEARD THROUGH THE DOORS.

EILEEN

Welcome, I'll get the drinks in.

DALJIT

I'll help

EILEEN

It's ok Daljit, I've got this.

OCEAN

Don't bother. We're not staying.

BRIAN

We just got here, Ocean.

EILEEN

Reframe right? drink, yeah. Nice. Is there an issue?

OCEAN

Starters: Noise, smoke inhalation, negative atmosphere, an off-room presence…

BRIAN
Babe…

OCEAN

You don't need to take my coat, Brian. Look, we will meet these good people again, not here, not in this house.

Come, Brian. Daljit, you can stay with Eileen if you wish, but we can offer you a lift. Not far out of our way I think.

EILEEN

It's fine, Daljit

DALJIT

I don't like to leave you

EILEEN

Another time, another place. It's fine. Really.

DOOOR CLOSES AS THEY ALL LEAVE. EILEEN ALONE WITH THE THUD OF THE TV. SHE GOES UPSTAIRS. A TELEPHONE RINGS DOWNSTAIRS BUT IS UNANSWERED. SHE WALKS INTO WARDROBE ROOM OFF BEDROOM, UNDRESSING FROM EVENING CLOTHES PICKS UP AN ITEM OF CLOTHING

That hat, I didn't know I still had it


LAYS DOWN ON THE BED IN A REVERIE, THE CRICKET THEME TUNE IS HEARD AS IN A DREAM

Seem so long ago know, how many seasons…

THE MURMUR OF VOICES, THE SOUND OF CHURCH BELLS, THE DISTINCTIVE THUD OF CRICET BALL ON BAT, APPLAUSE…

COMMENTATOR

…seasons unchanging yet unlike any other, here at this most English of cricket grounds we are witnessing something special. Now that is unusual at a county ground these days, a six on the stroke of lunch, well-earned Herbert Vane, leaving the square and making straight for the pavilion. Something special on the menu today…

HERBERT AND BRIAN ENTER THE PAVILION, BANTERING WITH TEAM
MATES

BRIAN

No, Carly, pies are so last season, I think you'll have the
avocado salad

VANE

I know what I like, I like what I know

BRIAN

You don't know what's good for you, Vane, man

VANE

You are so wrong, John. I like what is on the menu today
Baptiste. What is your name, Darling?

EILEEN

I don't think you should be speaking to the Head Chef that
way, Mr Vane.

VANE

Head chef? Mr Vane? Did you hear that, brother?

BRIAN
The Head Chef is right, you should treat people with the
respect they deserve.

VANE

I thought I was

EILEEN

Eileen, call me Eileen. Do try the avocado salad

VANE
Eileen. Yes, Eileen, I'll get the salad.

EXT / INT ACOUSTIC - EILEEN'S REVERIE IS INTERRUPTED BY
TELEPHONE AUDIBLE OVER THE TV DOWNSTAIRS. SHE DESCENDS STAIRS
AND ENTERS THE ROOM. THE TV, STILL PLAYING THE CRICKET MATCH
LOOP IS TURNED UP OVER THE TELEPHONE.

EILEEN

Answer the phone Herbert, turn off the TV, I'll make you
something to eat. Please.

THE NOISE CONTINUES

EILEEN

Herbert, for my sake, please , remember how we used to be

THERE IS KNOCKING AT THE DOOR, AT FIRST POLITE, THEN INCESSANT, FINALLY AUDIBLE ABOVE TV. EILEEN ANSWERS

EILEEN

Daljit

DALJIT ENTERS AND ADDRESSES VANE

Eileen is coming with me

EILEEN

Am I?

DALJIT

TO VANE Eileen is coming with me. TO EILEEN You are coming with me. Get some things. Now.

THEY GO UPSTAIRS, PACK A BAG FROM WARDROBE, THE NOISE DOWNSTAIRS CONTINUES. THE EXTERNAL DOOR CLOSES, CAR DRIVES OFF.

VANE IN ROOM, FINALLY TURNS OFF TV. SILENCE. LIGHTS A CIGARETTE AND OPENS CAN.

VANE

Eileen

HE OPENS EXTERNAL DOOR

Eileen.


4

**INT – EVENING, FRONT ROOM, HOUSE OF DALJIT AND RAMESH DASS, LEEDS**

EILEEN

It wasn't always there. We had it put in. House upgrade. Proceeds of Herb's first international call up.

OCEAN

You installed a hatch in your house? What were you trying to say?

EILEEN

I wasn't trying to say anything. We thought it was a good idea.

OCEAN

It isn't

DALJIT CALLING OUT TO RAMESH IN ADJACENT KITCHEN

How is the dinner coming along, Ramesh. Do you need any help?

**RAMESH DASS**  ENTERING ROOM

Would you like to come through ladies, help yourselves.

EILEEN

This is the most glorious buffet I have seen since…

OCEAN

Have you considered knocking the wall down, kitchen diner?

RAMESH

No

DALJIT

This is how we like it. Do start.

EILEEN

This is amazing

RAMESH

That is amazing from you, Eileen. Your catering is legendary

EILEEN

How would you describe this style?

DALJIT

Leeds Bangladesh? Wouldn't you agree, dearest?

RAMESH

You express it so well, Daljit darling. I will leave you ladies now.

EILEEN
Is that man a saint?

OCEAN
This is a man free zone this evening ladies. Enjoy. THEY ENJOY
THE BUFFET What does Ramesh do on ladies nights?

DALJIT

I don't know. BEAT He has a study. Reads, writes, listens to
music and drama. Brian?

OCEAN
Brian is training. And he of who we do not speak?

EILEEN

We can speak of Herbert. I don't have a problem with that.
This food is to live for.

OCEAN

That is how you and Herbert met isn't it? That's a good buffet
topic, first meetings. Who first, Daljit darling. You and
Ramesh.

DALJIT

Leeds University. Medical school. Sorry, not exactly
interesting.

OCEAN

Interesting, very. Exact, no. I think you are a dark horse,
Daljit.

EILEEN
Me too. I feel I've known Daljit for ages but then I don't.
I'm going to ask Ramesh.

OCEAN

We said no men this evening, ladies. Go on, Daljit. When,
where, how. Spicy.

DALJIT

We met in a night club. You know Leeds nightlife.

OCEAN

You don't drink

DALJIT

Do you have to drink to have a good time, dance?

OCEAN
Wasn't what I meant, no offence.

RAMESH  ENTERS FROM KITCHEN WITH MORE PLATES FOR BUFFET

Life is a banquet, beautiful but soon over. Everything
alright, ladies? Enjoy. It is your evening. RETURNS TO HIS
KITCHEN / STUDY.

OCEAN

He seems a wise man, your man. Go on, Daljit.

DALJIT

Night club, dancing. Suavey old Ramesh comes up to me, said do
you want to dance. I said I already am. He said anyone can
dance, only you can dance with me.

OCEAN

That's his nickname, Suavey?

EILEEN

Nice one

OCEAN

So you didn't meet at University. You met in a night club.
Nothing wrong with that.

EILEEN

I don't think she said there was.

DALJIT

I was studying medicine. He was studying sports sciences -
combines medicine, psychology, coaching. Came over on a
cricket tour from Bangladesh. When his playing days were over
he had a choice, coaching or cooking

EILEEN

Obs he chose both

OCEAN

Did he choose you or you him?

DALJIT

Talking of night clubs and dancing let's have some music.
Smartphones on the table, each of us chooses a track to
accompany each of the dishes from our buffet. Deal?

MUSIC. THEY DON'T HEAR DOORBELL. OCEAN'S TRACK IS INTERRUPTED
BY RING TONE.

OCEAN PICKS UP

I told you this is a ladies night. What do you want Brian?

BRIAN ON PHONE

Ocean, you said pick me up after training. I've an early start
tomorrow.

OCEAN

Where are you now?

BRIAN
Outside. I've been ringing the door bell. Thought I must have
the wrong venue.

DALJIT HAS REPLACED THE DANCE MUSIC ON THE PHONES WITH RAGA
CLASSICAL MUSIC.

DALJIT

Ask whoever it is to come over.

IMMEDIATELY THERE IS A TAP ON THE DOOR

RAMESH APPEARS TO ANSWER IT

RAMESH
TO LADIES This is like something out of *Noises Off*. OPENING
DOOR Welcome

BRIAN ENTERS, SPEAKS DIRECTLY TO OCEAN

BRIAN
Babe, it's one o clock…

OCEAN

Brian Baby, I lost track of time

BRIAN
…in the morning.

OCEAN

Easy, baby

BRIAN

Have you been drinking?

DALJIT

We don't drink do we girls

BRIAN

I'm opening the batting tomorrow. Someone has to stay
disciplined.

RAMESH

An opener? I knew it.

BRIAN

I thought this was ladies night

RAMESH

It was, is. MOVING HIM OFF TO KITCHEN AREA Come into my study,
friend,  I mean kitchen. Let me fix you one of my specials.
You'll be 94 not out by the lunch interval. No worries.


5

**EXT ACOUSTIC  - DAYTIME THE COUNTY GROUND**

APPLAUSE, SHOUTS OF 'WELL PLAYED YOUNG MAN' A BRASS BAND
STARTS UP

COMMENTATOR

With star opener Brian Baptiste on the verge of a century our
lunchtime feature today should steady us all. Or perhaps that
should be nearly all. Yes, it is a trip down memory lane, but
the past can be a difficult place to live in. I'm talking of
course of that other star opener, a partner once of todays
hero Brian aka John Baptiste, Herbert Vane. Remember him?
Today we look back at the highlights of Vane's career and ask
where is he now? The hard questions that can no longer be
avoided…

INT ACOUSTIC TV IS ON IN HERBERT VANE'S ROOM. COMMENTATOR
CONTINUES

…Is that a career to date or a sell by

VANE IS RUMMAGING IN A FRIDGE

Is that a beer to date or a sell by. HE OPENS A CAN. I think
that one has been answered, Herb, my son.

HE RETURNS WITH DRINK AND UNMUTES TV

HERBERT ON TV IN A  CLIP FROM EARLER INTERVIEW
… I don't see myself as a hero. In cricket there is always, by
definition someone at the other end, you cannot achieve these
victories alone. HERBERT IN ROOM There is always someone at
the other end. Please. HE MUTES TV AGAIN AND OPENS ANOTHER CAN
THEN UNMUTES TV TO REJOIN THE INTERVIEW CLIPS

COMMENTATOR

..the modern cricketer, away from home so much, Herbert Vane
you have spoken before of your wife Eileen, without whom…

HERBERT

Yeah, yeah, yeah. Where is the remote? Must be something
worthwhile on…

COMMENTATOR

This is a sport of timing. The time lapse of the ball leaving
the bowler's hand and arriving at the batsmen's end is not
even a second but it can seem a lifetime to those who…

HERBERT HAS LEFT THE TV AND IS RUMMAGING IN AN EMPTY FRIDGE

Where is the remote Where is..? SHOUTS OUT Eileen, Eileen

COMMENTATOR
And with those questions over the boundary, we return to the
action with Brian Baptiste taking the field again, perhaps
only one shot away from….

HERBERT RETURNS TO THE ROOM AND PULLS OUT THE TV PLUG.
SILENCE.

THEN SOUND OF PHONE RINGING. HERBERT BLUNDERS AROUND TRYING TO
FIND THE RECEIVER. EVENTUALLY PICKS UP

VOICE OF PERCIVAL SAMUELS ON TELEPHONE AS BEFORE

Herb, Mr Herbert Vane?

HERBERT PULLS PHONE SOCKET PLUG

SILENCE.

**EXT / INT DAY  OCEAN AND BRIAN'S SUITE, ANTIGUA**

FADE UP SOUND OF WAVES, STEEL BAND,

**STAFANIE**

Let me refresh your cocktail, madam

OCEAN

Down the hatch

STAFANIE

Sir?

BRIAN

I'm fine. Thanks

SILENT SIP

BRIAN

Yeah, Guilty

OCEAN

Guilty! You are here with this beautiful woman, in beautiful place, this place of our heritage, where we are one and you use a word like that. Don't make me think I have made the wrong choice, Mr Baptiste. Guilty. About?

BRIAN

Carly, I mean Herb, Vane.

OCEAN

Who?

BRIAN
Eileen's ex

OCEAN

Ex, exactly. Exactly why are we -  here, anywhere - discussing that loser.

BRIAN

He wasn't always.

OCEAN

He is now

BRIAN
Maybe you are right

OCEAN
No maybe, baby.

BRIAN

You, sea, paradise. Want to go up, woman, change before
dinner?

OCEAN

We can go up. No need to change anyone, anything.

STAFANIE

Telephone call for you, sir.

OCEAN       .

Sir will take it later.


7

**EXT ACOUSTIC - DAY THE COUNTY CRICKET GROUND**

COMMENTATOR

Ladies and Gentlemen, you may be surprised to know some
factors are even beyond the control of our generous host today
Sir Percival Samuels. Apologies for the delayed start. Our
gentlemen v players fixture will be underway in no time

RAMESH

Sun after rain, as arranged. And the delay means Mr Vane will
be on time.

EILEEN

You aren't going to do some alignment of the Gods type thing
are you Ramesh?

RAMESH

Match fixing is illegal. And you, Eileen, get back in the
marquee. I don't want you visible. Yet.

COMMENTATOR

Welcome ladies and gentlemen to our special match today at
this legendary ground, today at the invitation of our host Sir
Percival Samuels. A household name needs no introduction but I
should mention all the nonplaying players today, the
administrators, the caterers, who give up their time and make
everything possible. The real beneficiaries are the inner city
Kidz who we encourage to take up our noble sport and keep
themselves out of trouble. And in now, another man who needs
no introduction Mr Herbert Vane…

THE APPLAUSE IS MIXED AS HERBERT STUMBLES OUT OF THE CATERING
TENT

COMMENTATOR

Enjoy this moment, ladies and gentlemen, a charitable match to
be played in the best traditions of our game. Do feel free to
leave the catering area..

EILEEN  COMING FORWARD

Herbert, it's Eileen, Herbert, for god's sake, you should let
me take care of those whites

HERBERT VANE STOPS MOMENTARILY TO SWIG FROM A BOTTLE OF WINE
AND DRAW ON HIS CIGARETTE

I'm going out to bat, out of my way

RAMESH  TO EILEEN

Eileen, don't dear, stay in the marquee. I've got this.

TO HERBERT VANE

Good afternoon, sir. My name is Ramesh. Good luck sir

VANE

Luck?

RAMESH  WALKING WITH HERBERT

I think you are going to need more hands, sir, like those
pictures of the goddesses. Hands for the bottle, hands for the
tobacco, hands for the bat, hands to offer friendship

VANE STOPS FOR A BEAT WITH RAMESH THEN WALKS ON

Get lost

**INT / EXT THE SAME DAY  ROOM /   BALCONY OF OCEAN AND BRIAN'S
SUITE**

AUDIBLE BEYOND THE BALCONY: MUSIC, PALM TREES IN BREEZE, WAVES
IN NEAR DISTANCE, CHILDREN PLAYING BEACH CRICKET

OCEAN AND BRIAN KISSING THEN MOVING ONTO BALCONY TAKING IN THE
SCENE

OCEAN

The telephone calls, Brian. Who are they from, or to?

BRIAN

If you need to know, Ocean princess, I'll tell you. Trust me.
It's for us. Everything is.

OCEAN

We can't have secrets, you and I. You're my man. That's how it
is. Forever. Who is it? The coach, the selectors? I get it.
Herbert Vane. Do you owe him something. Has he got some hold
on you?

BRIAN

The only one who can ever have some hold on me is you. I can't
take my eyes off you.

OCEAN

Sometimes it's your job to take your eyes off me. I know it is
only for split seconds. Tell me or no more…

BRIAN

I don't owe anyone anything. Except you. Maybe I would be like
Vane without you. We reached the top together..

OCEAN

You are still there.

BRIAN
It's easier to slip than you know. One mistake, people talk,
you're too old, technique shot, you're playing for yourself
not the team…

OCEAN
Who did you call baby?

BRIAN
Eileen

OCEAN
Eileen. The loser's wife?

BRIAN

I tried to see Vane, get him centred, going nowhere. I told
Eileen I'd been in touch with a cricketing charity.

OCEAN

Charity. We don't do charity.

BRIAN

We do second chances

OCEAN

What is this charity?

BRIAN

Celebs, TV, music people who are into cricket. Gentlemen v
players, scratch club games together for good causes, you know
the sort of thing.

OCEAN

I don't. You are a gentleman, and a player. You command good
money. The cause is us. Keep it that way.

BRIAN
UK time. Herbert will be on his way out to the middle now.

OCEAN

This is our time, honey. Celebration time. Come on.

THEY MOVE BACK INTO ROOM FROM BALCONY. KISSES INTERRUPTED BY
PHONE. OCEAN PICKS UP ON FIRST RING

OCEAN
Who is this. This is our time. I see. Yes, of course. TO
BAPTISTE. For you, head coach.

**EXT - COUNTY GROUND THE SAME DAY**

COMMENTATOR

The long walk back is a traditional phrase in cricket, I must say that was rather a long walk out. I must say the washing powder manufacturers seemed to have pulled out of Mr Vane's sponsorship...markets can be very fluid I observe…

BACK IN THE MARQUEE RAMESH, EILEEN AND DALJIT

DALJIT

At least he is here. That is really something. How did that happen?

EILEEN

I'm not entirely sure. I wondered if you or Ramesh knew anything about it, or absent friends

RAMESH

It is simply magical to see him out, I mean out in the middle, in the fresh air.

COMMENTATOR

Nevertheless, the expression fans want to hear today is - Herbert Vane to take strike. He is setting up in the time-honoured fashion…

VANE IS AT THE CREASE MARKING THE GROUND WITH HIS BAT

COMMENTATOR

..and how sporting, our host, the man at the other end comes forward to welcome Vane to the crease. I wonder what the sportsmen will be saying to each other at this time..

SIR P S   TO VANE

Well done old boy, nice to have you with us

VANE'S RESPONSE IS OBSCURED BY FEEDBACK NOISE FROM THE P A SYSTEM

COMMENTATOR

…bowler turning at his mark, in now past the umpire, the moment of truth, seems like an eternity

**EXT - THE SAME DAY, THE BEACH IN FRONT OF OCEAN AND BRIAN'S APARTMENT**

THE GENTEEL SOUND FROM THE ENGLISH COUNTY GROUND MERGES INTO THE SOUNDS OF A CARIBBEAN BEACH, SURF, MUSIC, PALM TREES, MORE WAVES INTO OCEAN'S DREAM

OCEAN

Brian, where are you Brian man?

THWACK OF CRICKET BALL ON BAT, COMMENTATOR LOUDLY OVER SOUND SYSTEM

Classy, another century for England's Brian Baptiste, the winning six for him  - how often have we heard that recently - and the winning score for his team

OCEAN

Brian

BRIAN

You asleep when I  score a 100, babe?

OCEAN

You score them so often, not that I'm complaining, boss

PAPARAZZI, PRESS, PHOTOGRAPHERS ARE GATHERING AROUND THEM, JOSTLING

Brian, yeah man, nice, like it, hey Ocean, let's have you and Brian together, bat, bikini, beach, loving it, what do you say Ocean, quote for the run machine

OCEAN

That isn't what I would call him

**EXT - THE SAME DAY - ENGLISH COUNTY GROUND**

THE BEACH SCENE DISSOLVES TO SILENCE, SOUND OF CRICKET BALL
FLYING THROUGH THE AIR, FOLLOWED BY THE CRASH OF UPROOTED
FLYING STUMPS

EILEEN

Jesus, Mary and Joseph, what just happened, Ramesh what
happened?

DALJIT

It will be alright, Eileen, that can happen to anyone

COMMENTATOR

Is there a worse sound in the world, the knell of ball on
stumps, no shot played, of course it can happen to anyone,
anytime, but this isn't anyone, anytime

EILEEN

Ramesh, you agreed this was a good idea, a way back, a way
forward, now what

RAMESH
It must have been meant to happen. There are so many positives

EILEEN

Such as

RAMESH

He left the room

EILEEN

You are responsible for this. Now what?

RAMESH
He must leave the crease

COMMENTATOR

Someone told me of a President of a non-test playing country
who didn't concede, but a clean bowled batsman not walking,
what is the world coming to. I do not believe what is
happening, or not. Hang on, something is coming through on the
stump microphone, I hope it is not going to offend our
listeners around the globe

SIR P S   VIA STUMP MICROPHONE

Bad luck, old sport, I think the convention is now you walk
back to the pavilion. Reflexes not what they were, what?
Happens to the best of us. Now steady on, old sport

COMMENTATOR
The batsman has raised his bat, no that is most untraditional,
no….I hope medics will not be called for… to make matters
worse one of the spectators has run on to the field, I don't
believe what I am seeing, that's former Bangladeshi opener
Ramesh Dass…

VANE  SHOUTING SLURRING ALMOST UNINTELLIGIBLY PICKED UP BY
STUMP MICROPHONE

You too, you B...

MICROPHONE CUT


12


**INT  - EVENING AT RAMESH AND DALJIT'S LEEDS HOME**

PLEASANT ATMOSPHERE, LIGHT MUSIC, CLINK OF GLASSES

DALJIT

Ocean and Brian, welcome, *Namaskar,* welcome back it seems a
century since you were last here. What's changed for you guys?
You look like a million dollars.

RAMESH

That's probably what they – he  – earns now. CPL, Caribbean
Premier League. Not like my day, play for your country,
payment enough.

EILEEN
That's a very un-Ramesh type remark

DALJIT
Come on, Eileen, a million dollars!

OCEAN
That's a very un-Daljit remark, have things changed for you

RAMESH
Let's leave the ladies. Retire, Brian. To the kitchen – study.

Tell me what's changed, what stays the same.

DALJIT
Suavey old Ramesh, retiring to the parlour

THE MEN LEAVE TO NEXT ROOM

OCEAN SIPS HER DRINK

Mmm, this is lovely Daljit, you must tell me how you mix it

DALJIT

We all have our mysteries

OCEAN

Ladies, let's do me first, Married, famous, well on all the islands..

DALJIT

Rich

OCEAN
Getting there

EILEEN

I'm pleased for you

DALJIT
That's big of you

OCEAN

Why do you say that, Daljit? Whatever, let's do Eileen

EILEEN
single, broke

DALJIT
Alive

EILEEN

Herbert would never have hurt me

OCEAN
So he's forced himself in the conversation, yeah

DALJIT
Alcohol can do strange things to people. It isn't that they act out of character. They transmogrify.

OCEAN

Right, and you Doc

RAMESH AND BRIAN RE-ENTER

RAMESH

What a beautiful smile, Daljit darling..

OCEAN

What have you two been drinking, Brian?

RAMESH

I was telling Brian I'm the richest man in the world


13

**INT  - EVENING   BROADCASTING STUDIO LONDON**

JAZZY SIGNATURE TUNE

SIR  P S

Good evening and welcome. Folks, we have a special show live in London this evening. Take guard, you are about to be bowled over, knocked for six, , select your own metaphor, even if  - what is wrong with you - you don't love cricket, maidens and gentlemen, in next at number one if you get where I'm coming from a very special guest, wheels down from Antigua SNATCH OF CARIBBEAN CRICKET THEME TUNE, SIR BUILDING OVER STUDIO APPLAUSE

and the man who needs no introduction so he isn't going to get one, right here in St Johns Wood, Mr Herbert Vane. Mind the step, Herb.

SNATCH OF CRICKET THEME TUNE, MIXED APPLAUSE PLAYS VANE IN OVER SOUND MONTAGE OF CRICKET SHOTS AND CROWD NOISE

SIR P S

You made it

VANE

Why wouldn't I

SIR P S

Help yourself to a drink. Settle in for the show.

CLINK OF BOTTLE, GLASS, ICE

SIR P  S

Down the hatch, on the rocks

VANE

Up yours

VANE REFILLING

Join me?

SIR  P  S

Herbert Vane offering me my liquor, on my prog, live radio, ladies and gentlemen. Bit early in the show for me, old sport.


Look, smooth to have you on the show. We heard  - and for those of you following us on the web  - saw on the introductory package some of your greatest hits from the past. I said you need no introduction but *tempus fugit* some of our younger listeners might only know of your epic partnership with Brian Baptiste that summer at Lords, that summer forever known as that summer. Let's hear it again

IT IS THE SAME LOOP AS VANE PLAYS ENDLESSLY IN HIS ROOM

AS SOUND CLIP REACHES THE END SIR  P S  WAITS FOR VANE TO COME IN BUT HE ONLY CONTINUES TO POUR DRINKS

SIR P S

That's your cue Herbert. You know the score.

VANE

Play the clip again.

SIR  P S

Of course I would never criticise a man for not moving on, seeking new grounds but would you like to tell the ladies and gentlemen what you have been doing since, that summer, that game, those celebrations?

VANE  THE CLINKING GLASS

This

EXT / INT SOUND SWITCH TO EILEEN AND OCEAN LISTENING TOGETHER AT OCEAN'S CARRIBEAN ROOM

EILEEN

Why did he agree to go on?

OCEAN

Free drinks, fee for more drinks. SHE RAISES HER COCKTAIL Down the hatch

EILEEN

It's true, people will forget who he was, is

OCEAN

Including him

EILEEN

I don't think I can listen anymore SHE OPENS THE WINDOWS TO
THE SEA

OCEAN

We can hit the beach anytime Eileen. Sit down, Brian will be
on in a sec. Save the day. Again.

ON RADIO CARIBBEAN CRICKET THEME TUNE STARTS UP, APPLAUSE IN
STUDIO, APPLAUSE FROM STUDIO CROWD, APPLAUSE FROM ON AIR
PACKAGE OF BRIAN HITTING SIXES

SIR P S

Herb, thanks for coming on. The pleasure is all mine. Next man
in, it has to be, don't call him John, he performs his own
miracles, Mr Brian Baptiste.

BRIAN SETTLING
Thank you kindly, Sir, too kind, thank you people, how you
doing Herb mate.  Cheers all.

SIR P S

Brian, welcome, let me offer you a drink. Gosh, could someone
open another bottle.

BRIAN

I'm good, thank you sir. I carry my own drinks these days.

SIR P S

Tell us what you have there

BRIAN

It's a special drink concocted by two friends of mine, medics
at Leeds University, secret formula, herbal, naturally,
guaranteed success on - and off - the field

SIR P S  ON AIR]

OCEAN OFF AIR, SIMULTANEOUSLY]

Isn't he something

SIR P S

Listeners, I need to give you the scene, Brian Baptiste is wearing more logos than a 1970s formula one driver, and the snazziest get up, what happened to the whites, Brian?

BRIAN

Caribbean Premier League, sorry right off the Airbus, no time to change.

SIR P S

Save laundering the old whites, what Herb. Let me bring you back in. Actually let's stay with you, Brian. Look everyone wants to hear the story of how you and Herb Vane first came together.

VANE

I don't.

SIR P S

Hardly sporting, Herbert.

VANE
I didn't know Baptiste was coming on. If I had, I wouldn't. I've had enough.

FEEDBACK SCREECH AS VANE ATTEMPTS TO REMOVE HIS MICROPHONE

SIR P S

Sit down, Mr Vane. We've all had enough. People, this is live radio. No one wants to see a man, a legend, down. Or a man become a legend again for all the wrong reasons.

I am going to issue a challenge, best intentions, right here, right now. Everyone knows cricket, life itself, can pivot on the toss of a coin. Here it is.

ASIDE
I'm sorry I've no cash on me, can someone bring me a coin, pound, sovereign , whatever..

TO EVERYONE ON AIR

It's a sporting challenge, Herbert Vane, are you man enough to take it. Heads or tails?

EILEEN OFF AIR

Take it.

OCEAN
Eileen girl, let me fix your cocktail. We don't know what the challenge is yet.

EILEEN

I do. Banana and pineapple. No rum.

SIR PS TO VANE ON AIR

Heads you give up the drink, tails you can't. Secret challenge, you and I, Herbert old sport. We go back long enough. I'll help you, either way. I've been there. Love of the sport, love of the country that was so proud you represented them. You man enough?

VANE
What makes you think I need any help. Anyway, it wouldn't be you I'd be asking.

SIR P S

Anyway, heads or tails, Vane, your call.

BRIAN

Let me fix your drink, Herb, drink from the same glass, wouldn't be the first time. No one is looking.

EILEEN  OFF AIR

Nice one, Brian

SIR  P S  ON AIR

Old times, new times, as they say, it's up in the air THE COIN IS TOSSED Don't run yourself out

VANE  DRINKS, PUTS DOWN GLASS

Heads

SIR P S

I love live radio

THEME MUSIC, OUT


14

**INT — DAY AT DOOR OF RAMESH AND DALJIT HOUSE, LEEDS**

DALJIT

Do stay, I'm cooking

BRIAN

I can't. No offence.

DALJIT
Is this where it is customary to say non taken?

BRIAN
I have to check in. Tonight flight to Dubai and Mumbai, then
Melbourne, then Auckland, then Antigua.

DALJIT
I˙hope you offset

RAMESH  JOINING THEM

Come in, out of the rain. He's here.

DALJIT

Plenty of homecooked food. Sounds like it will be some time
before you get some.

BRIAN

I haven't come to see him. This is for you.

RAMESH

The old plain brown envelope job, eh. Not the sort of thing we
do, friend.

BRIAN
It's for you Ramesh. I want you, you and Daljit, to understand
even more. Don't show it to Carly, I mean Herbert, at least
until the day after tomorrow

DALJIT

Intrigue. Intriguing. I must get back to my cooking.

RAMESH
Tell me what it is

BRIAN

Open it. Now

RAMESH OPENS THE PACKAGE

RAMESH

A VHS tape

BRIAN
I figured you'd still have a player. See you, friend.

HERBERT VANE FROM INSIDE THE HOUSE

Who is that at the door? Eileen?

RAMESH GOES INSIDE  TO HERBERT
A friend

ENTERS KITCHEN

Everything under control darling?

DALJIT
Dinner will be served presently

VANE
Mmm, fresh herbs. Be easier to serve if you had one of those
hatches installed. What have you there?

RAMESH

Nothing

VANE
No one at the door delivers nothing. You two, always cooking.

DALJIT
Nutrition, I mean dinner, and early night for you Mr Vane.

VANE
And you?

DALJIT
Dinner, theatre, clubbing. Typical Leeds night. Don't wait up.

LATER, CLUNK OF VHS TAPE ENTERING MACHINE

RAMESH

I hope this isn't a bootleg of *Noises Off*

DALJIT
As if Brian would do such a thing.  How did Mr Baptiste know
you would still have a VHS?

RAMESH

Players never lose their class, darling

COMMENTATOR ON TAPE, OLD STYLE

Great players have to start somewhere and it might be here.
You join us today at the county ground, for this special
report on the young colts, are these the heroes of tomorrow.

A big day for the boys in white, the scouts are on the lookout, success here could lead to travels and riches beyond dreams. Here they are, the spin of the coin and in they go. Good luck young sirs.

Two exceptionally talented young openers here, timing, communication, the future calls, remember these names Herbert Vane and Brian Baptiste

ON TAPE HERBERT SHOUTING]

No

SIMULTANEOUSLY WITH RAMESH AND DALJIT IN THEIR ROOM]

No

COMMENTATOR

No one saw that coming. It is young Baptiste. The more senior boy Vane took responsibility, his shout of No could be heard in Adelaide, young Baptiste is running to the wrong end, he is at the point of no return. There is no run there. Vane has set off himself, he is running towards the danger end. The throw is in. Curtains. Young Vane is still running, towards the pavilion.

THE TAPE RUNS ON AND CLUNKS OUT. SILENCE

15

**EXT / INT DAY – OCEAN'S SUITE IN CARIBBEAN, LATER**

DOOR BUZZER

STAFANIE (BUTLER / CONCIERGE) Special delivery for Ms Williams – Baptiste. Timed.

OCEAN  CALLING FROM SEA FACING BALCONY

Is that the butler, Eileen? I don't think I can handle any more champagne.

EILEEN

What do I call you? I can't very well say butler.

STAFANIE

My name is Stafanie. I will need a signature.

EILEEN

Thank you. TO OCEAN It's Stafanie. You will have to sign, Ocean.

OCEAN ARRIVES AND SIGNS

EILEEN GIVES STAFANIE A TIP.

Thank you, Stafanie.

DOOR CLOSES.

OCEAN
Really it is addressed to us both Eileen Vane - are you going
to do something about that name, honey ? - c/o Ocean Williams
- Baptiste.

You open, girl. Too small for me.

EILEEN AND OCEAN LAUGH

EILEEN

Cricket tours are so long these days. OPENING OUTER PACKAGE

That logo, seen it before, where….

OCEAN

What is that, woman?

EILEEN

Memory stick

OCEAN

Stick it in

EILEEN TYPES CLOSE THE OPEN SPREADSHEET ON HER PC AND
KEYSTROKES THE MEMORY STICK IN. MUSIC STARTS AS PROGRAMME
OPENS - IT IS THE THEME TUNE OF P.S'S RADIO / WEB SHOW SEQUE
INTO CRICKET THEME USED TO PLAY IN BRIAN BAPTISTE

SIR P S  VIA SCREEN ON EILEEN'S LAPTOP

Folks, do not adjust your set…

EILEEN  COMMENTING ON WHAT SHE SEES ON SCREEN

That is it. The logo. Sir Percival Samuel's charity, it was
everywhere, the marquee bunting,  the sports ground flags, the
champagne marque..


SIR P S CONTINUING ON SCREEN

It doesn't get any better than this. And don't take old Percy
Samuels word for it. Here is the patronising, sorry I'll read
that again, our patron Brian - way isn't there a sir in front
of that name - Baptiste.

THERE IS A BEEP AS BRIAN HOLOGRAMS ONTO THE SCREEN

BRIAN

People, I'm sorry I am not with you in person today..

OCEAN   COMMENTING OFF SCREEN
Tell me about it Brian babe. Look at the backdrop Eileen,
didn't know the boy was that IT savvy.  You'd think he was in
Dubai or something.

BRIAN   CONTINUING ON SCREEN

If it's Monday it must be Melbourne, or if it's Friday it must
be Dubai, one thing is for sure, this is the game at its best.
You might see classier cricket someplace else in the world –
after all this is one franchise I'm not in – you won't see it
played in better spirit. Watch this people, this is it.
Respect. HE BEEPS OFF. CONTINUING ON FULL SCREEN

COMMENTATOR   ON SCREEN

Indeed we would love to have Brian Baptiste in person playing
today but he has set the scene so generously. Welcome to the
perfect setting that is the county ground for this charity
match curated by the Sir Percival Samuels Foundation. Let's
meet the teams. Introduced by Captain Herbert Vane – excuse me
while I don my sunglasses, those whites are dazzlers – it is
the Urban Regenerates XI. I love that slogan some wag has
attached to the bunting over the catering marquee ' be nice to
us, we are vulnerable.' And those men in cravats, roared on by
Mr Suave himself, the Ramesh Tigers XI. Let's hear it. Thank
you to all, sportsmen, celebrities, both in some cases, for
giving up their time.

SIR P S   ON SCREEN

I personally selected them so there would be no competition
from daytime television this day, they are all here

EILEEN

Please move it on

COMMENTATOR

At the stroke of lunch the match is finely balanced. One hopes
teams will be taking refreshments in an equally  balanced and
responsible way

OCEAN

Business opportunity there for you, Eileen…

EILEEN

Look there's Daljit, in the catering marquee.

OCEAN

All on her own, these so called gentlemen scoffing all the grub and necking all the booze

EILEEN

Darling Daljit. Hey Ocean, can you move this to close up. Yes, it's Daljit now with Ramesh

OCEAN

And your ex.

EILEEN

Freeze the frame. What is that logo on Herbert's drink?

OCEAN

I thought we'd moved on from that.

EILEEN

Blow that up. There.

OCEAN

I recognise that. It's the logo plastered all over Brian's kit. That health drink marketed by Ramesh. Brian must be making him a fortune.

EILEEN
That way round?

Look, it's Daljit and Ramesh, they've done their own catering, food and drink

OCEAN
What's new?

EILEEN
Herbert is with them. Herbert is with them.

OCEAN

Let's keep this moving TAPS SCREEN FORWARD

COMMENTATOR ON SCREEN

I am not making this up, is history repeating itself? The final ball of the final over, 6 to win, the bowler is at his mark, it is - who else could it be - Herbert Vane on strike, the ball is released..

EILEEN

Ocean, move it forward. Now.

OCEAN
Whatever you say, girl

COMMENTATOR   SPEAKING OVER SOUNDS OF CROWDS, BRASS BAND, FIREWORKS, CHAMPAGNE POPS

Hardly original perhaps but this is vintage Sir Percival Samuels, as classic as the ample champagne that carries his marque The red Routemaster glides forward, the sides of the bus where you would normally see advertisements emblazoned with the now familiar logos of the charity foundation.

The open top deck is a mix of red bus, cricket whites and green magnums open Grand Prix style. The wine is flowing as if the Karnaphuli River was in confluence with the Wharfe. They are all there, pride of place Sir Percival Samuels himself, flanked by the captains Ramesh of the tigers and Herbert of the Urban R…

EILEEN   OFF SCREEN

There. Look. Ramesh, centre, he is filling Herb's glass with that herb drink he invented, there is the logo, it is so clear

COMMENTATOR

It is Herbert Vane, raising his glass – I'll have what he is having – and, what sportsmanship, Ramesh immediately refills it, they toast each other. Herbert Vane has laid down his glass and taking out his mobile telephone. I expect he is taking a call from the board, his agent, an international franchise in a far away time zone, the sponsor of that drink…

IN THE BACKGROUND ABOVE THE SCENES ON LAPTOP SCREEN THE TELEPHONE IN ENTRANCE AREA OF OCEAN'S SUITE IS RINGING

STAFANIE ENTERS AND ANSWERS THE TELEPHONE

STAFANIE

Ms Williams – Baptiste's suite.

I see.

TO OCEAN

International. For you madam.

OCEAN

Brian, baby, what time is it where you are, what are you doing up so late on a match day eve…

Oh, I see. Mr Vane. Yes, Eileen is with me. I will see if she is available.

\Over    BBC

**Over**

Set in England and Antigua. The present

**Cast**

Herbert Vane

Eileen Vane

Brian Baptiste

Ocean Williams

Daljit Dass

Ramesh Dass

Sir Percival Samuels

Commentator(s)

Stafanie, paparazzi, theatre announcer…

# *Sight Test*

SCRIPT
YORKSHIRE *2020*

5' radiocast

*Drama King / Super - Over 2021*
www.johnkinginternational.co.uk

INTERIOR ACOUSTIC - INSIDE A SMALL,BARE
ENCLOSED ROOM TELEPHONE IS RINGING

EXT / INT ACOUSTIC  - FROM OUTSIDE THE ROOM
**HERBERT** OPENS DOOR, CRASHES INTO ROOM,
HURRIEDLY PUTS DOWN CARRIER BAG CLANKING WITH
CANS AND BOTTLES BUT DOES NOT REACH TELEPHONE
IN TIME, RINGING STOPS.

**HERBERT** OPENS CAN OF BEER, LIGHTS CIGARETTE.
SWITCHES ON RADIO- *CRICKET THEME TUNE*- RADIO
IMMEDIATELY VIOLENTLY TURNED OFF.

MORE BEER GULPS AND SMOKING. CAN CRUSHED ON
FLOOR.

### HERBERT

What? Do you have a problem? With me? Don't
think I should drink. Or smoke. Or exist? Let
me tell you something. I don't care. Whatever
image you have of me, had, whatever you wanted
me to be, it is because you wanted it. If I'm
lost, you are too. Golden boy, golden era, the
way you remember it, you remember yourself. Who
you were then. But I made it happen. I hit the
winning runs.  I'm the winner. You are
spectators. Anyone can shout at a TV.  I don't
care about…

TELEPHONE RINGS AGAIN.


### HERBERT

INTO TELEPHONE RECEIVER

Eileen?

**DALJIT**

VOICE ON TELEPHONE

Mr Herbert Vane please. Herbert, if I may call you that?

I have tried many times to reach you. I, we are trying to help you.

**HERBERT**

We? Who the hell are you?

**DALJIT**

VOICE ON PHONE

I have been asked to ring you, it isn't for me. It is for… Don't put the phone down.  Listen. Then I won't ring again. No one will stop you drinking.

**HERBERT**

I do what I want. What do you do?

**DALJIT**

VOICE ON PHONE

My name is Daljit Darsani, I am president of the Visually Impaired Cricket Association.

**HERBERT**

If you are trying to be amusing you are a failure.

**DALJIT**

VOICE ON PHONE

One of us is a failure. It isn't me.

**HERBERT**

Do you know who you are talking to? I am…

**DALJIT**

VOICE ON PHONE

I know who you used to be, Herbert. I don't think you know who you are now. Calling you was ill advised. I hear you are beyond recall.

**HERBERT**

Don't hang up. ANOTHER CAN OPENING, ANOTHER CIGARETTE.

Recall to what? Who did you say you were?

**DALJIT**

VOICE ON PHONE

I am Daljit Darsani, I represent the Visually Impaired Cricket Association.

**HERBERT**

Didn't think I'd heard of you.

**DALJIT**

VOICE ON PHONE

I was not aware of how rude you have become. I will contact the Board to rescind your spirit of cricket award. I do not see why our team should offer you a way back. I cannot envisage you as patron.

ENDS CALL

HERBERT IS LEFT WITH THE TONE OF THE PHONE.

**HERBERT**

No one hangs up on me.

INT / EXT- HERBERT LEAVES ROOM, SLAMS DOOR, OPENS CAR DOOR, REVS ENGINE, CRASHES GEARS, CAR SCREECHES TO HALT ON A GRAVEL DRIVEWAY. CAR DOOR OPENS. HE EXITS CAR AND BANGS ON HOUSE DOOR

**HERBERT**

Open this door. I'm not going anywhere.

**EILEEN**

OPENING A HEAVILY LOCKED DOOR

You haven't been going anywhere for a long time, darling. Which part of 'I never want to see you again' didn't you understand?

**DALJIT**

FROM INT ACOUSTIC.

Who is it, Eileen..?

HERBERT HAS MARCHED THROUGH ENTRANCE HALL ENTERING MAIN ROOM

**EILEEN**

INT ACOUSTIC

..No one, Daljit.

**HERBERT**

I will not be patronised. No one hangs up on me.

**EILEEN**

Left your manners wherever you are living these days, Herbert?  I asked Honorary President Darsani to explore a way back for you. Professionally.

**DALJIT**

We were looking for more of a cover driver than drink driver.

**HERBERT**

I'm...I'm...

**DALJIT**

Is sorry the word you are looking for, Mr Vane?

**EILEEN**

I'm sorry, Daljit. I shouldn't have involved you. SHE IS ON THE TELEPHONE Cab please, Adel, north Leeds. Soon as.

**DALJIT**

TO HERBERT

I know you had a long way to fall, Herbert, but..

**HERBERT**

I can stop drinking. Eileen, Mrs President.

**DALJIT**

...but can you stop being rude?

/

Sketch pre - *Over*

*Character development*

Herbert Vane.

Daljit Darsani, Hon President.

Eileen, ex Mrs Vane.

*Setting*:

North Leeds, the present

# Close of Play

The dreams we had as children.

August, another summer slipping away,

Birds high in the sky,

Wickets chalked on the dustbin.

My dad coming home from English Electric;

An over before tea,

Now dinner.

The past, maybe you just grow out of it.

# Picked

I'm just a kid like any other

Asking my Mum questions, looking for answers

That's how you learn, that's what I was told.

Where's Alfons now, I asked next morning before it got too hot to stay inside-

It felt a bit annoying to be cheated out of an uncle.

Why did he get on the wrong train-

He's just a kind like any other - was he all alone,

Weren't there any other nice people to help him?

Mum said not everyone was nice then in this city where she came from;

Situations can happen where some bad people do bad things.


Situations?

He was just a kid like any other.

Did someone pick on him?

Didn't anyone stand up for him?

Where did his train end up?




Why..?

Not every question has answers my Mum said.

I went outside to set up the wickets.

It was the longest day; that night the stars didn't
bother.

Upstairs

I practiced his name out loud for when I could meet
him:

Alfons

In time with the Strauss from the Schiedmayer below

Me and Alfons,

We're just kids like any other.

I couldn't sleep for the light.

SECOND GENERATION NETWORK

JBW

*For Alfons Hölzelmacher*
*Born Vienna 8.11.1930*
*Died Auschwitz 1944*

# Six!

90mph, 22 yards, 1 second

Ample time to remember

how you were last to picked in the school playground

almost behind you now

auctioned to play for millions

one second, an age

all you have to do is…

From Write Coach 2014

# The World Keeps on Spinning

There has never been a nuclear war between two cricket playing countries.

We live in a divided world, a dangerous world, an unpredictable world. We hear these assertions more and more following the political events of the Brexit referendum & the election of Mr Trump as president of the USA. Are these assertions actually true, and if so what is the answer?

Could the answer be cricket?

Imagine if Mr Trump and Mr Kim Jong-un of North Korea not only liked cricket but loved it would there be a diplomatic and potentially nuclear armed crisis in that region?

Cricket, a major sport in only 10 countries but currently played in over 100 has the potential to leave the back pages of the newspapers and the 'over to the sportsdesk' zone of the TV news to break into the international news in an uniquely positive way.

There are many current examples around the world of how this sport is making a positive difference and bringing individuals and groups together.

Here is a hat-trick of cricketing unity.

The countries of the former Yugoslavia descended into horrific wars. In 2014 Serbia became a key transit point on the Balkan refugee route into other parts of Europe, notably through Hungary or Croatia to Germany or Austria. With this route effectively closed thousands of refugees remained in Serbia. The majority of these are young men from Afghanistan and Pakistan. Cricketers. The Serbian Commissariat for refugees may not have a total understanding of the laws of cricket, they did have an understanding of its unifying and positive potential.

Vladimir Ninkovic, general secretary of the Serbian Cricket Federation now travels to the asylum centre in near Belgrade to organise matches twice a week. He said ' it gives them a few hours where they don't think of themselves as refugees or migrants, just good cricketers.' One of these refugees, Mr Sherzad said ' I am happy, I am alive and have friends, a job and a cricket team.'

President Trump has not yet followed the example of his predecessor Dwight D Eisenhower in attending an international cricket match but on the west coast of the USA there is an encouraging development. The Compton Cricket Club was founded in 1995 by Ted Hayes and Kay Haber following on from the LA Krickets, a team comprised of homeless men from Dome village Los Angeles. Young men joined the Compton Cricket Club as an alternative to gang activities in the neighbourhood. The welcome to Compton Cricket Club website prominently displays their code of ethics based on the laws and etiquettes unique to cricket.

The club has received polite shout outs from England opening batsman Nick Compton, Prince Edward and UK sports charities Cricket Without Boundaries, Lashings and Lord's Taverners.

In 1999 at the invitation of UK secretary of state for Northern Ireland Mo Mowlem they toured the province. They met Unionist leader David Trimble and

Sinn Fein's Gerry Adams. Shortly after their visit the Northern Ireland Peace agreements were concluded.

On a tour of Australia in 2011 they raised money for Queensland Flood relief and played the Aboriginal side Redfern All Blacks. Their journey is celebrated on a Bondi Beach mural.

The German Cricket Federation (DCB) became an affiliate of the International Cricket Council in 1991. When the CEO Brian Mantle took over the German DCB in 2012 there were 1,700 members registered in 70 teams. Now there are 4, 000 cricketers playing in 205 teams. Mr Mantle was approached by social workers realising the power of the game to integrate asylum seekers from Afghanistan and Pakistan. In 2016 Refugee Arifullah Jamal won an award for helping others and promoting cricket in Essen.

Further examples of the unifying capacity of this sport abound from the apparently most inhospitable continents to the more traditional cricketing regions such as England where you can see Gracie's the first

LGBT cricket club or watch a game in Rotherham across once suspicious communities. Jeremy Corbyn and Theresa May joined in their 60th birthday congratulations to BBC radio Test Match Special. Kevin Pietersen's bats now prominently feature the Save the Rhino sticker.

As global organisations including the EU, UN, WTO appear to lose reach perhaps it is time to learn new sets of acronyms – ICC, DCB, LBW and hope a cricket ball spins into Korea before something a lot more sinister.

Writer: John King, UK

2017

# The Real Thing

Sports may be subjects in themselves, metaphors of for example team players and individuals. Sports pictures ( Borg Vs McEnroe, Chariots of Fire, Downhill Racer, I, Tonya, The Loneliness of the Long Distance Runner, Moneyball, This Sporting Life, Touching the Void, White Men Can't Jump…) may transcend the sport to the world beyond.

Cricket scenes or references abound in TV series as diverse as The Avengers, Morse, even The West Wing and in films including The Dambusters, Hit for Six, Hope and Glory, Lagaan, Night Train to Munich , The Go- Between, Wondrous Oblivion

Full feature dramas with cricket as the dramatic subject include Playing Away, screenplay by Caryl Phillips 1987, Ayckbourne Time and Time Again , Bean The English Game , Gray Two Sundays

Bollywood's Chennai 60028 2007 and Victory 2009 illustrate Nandy's view 'cricket is an Indian game accidentally discovered by the British.'

In 1963 C L R James paraphrased Kipling's ' what do they know of England who only England know?' to ' what do they know of cricket who only cricket know?'

Documentary 2019

Cricket at Oxford from the film Accident

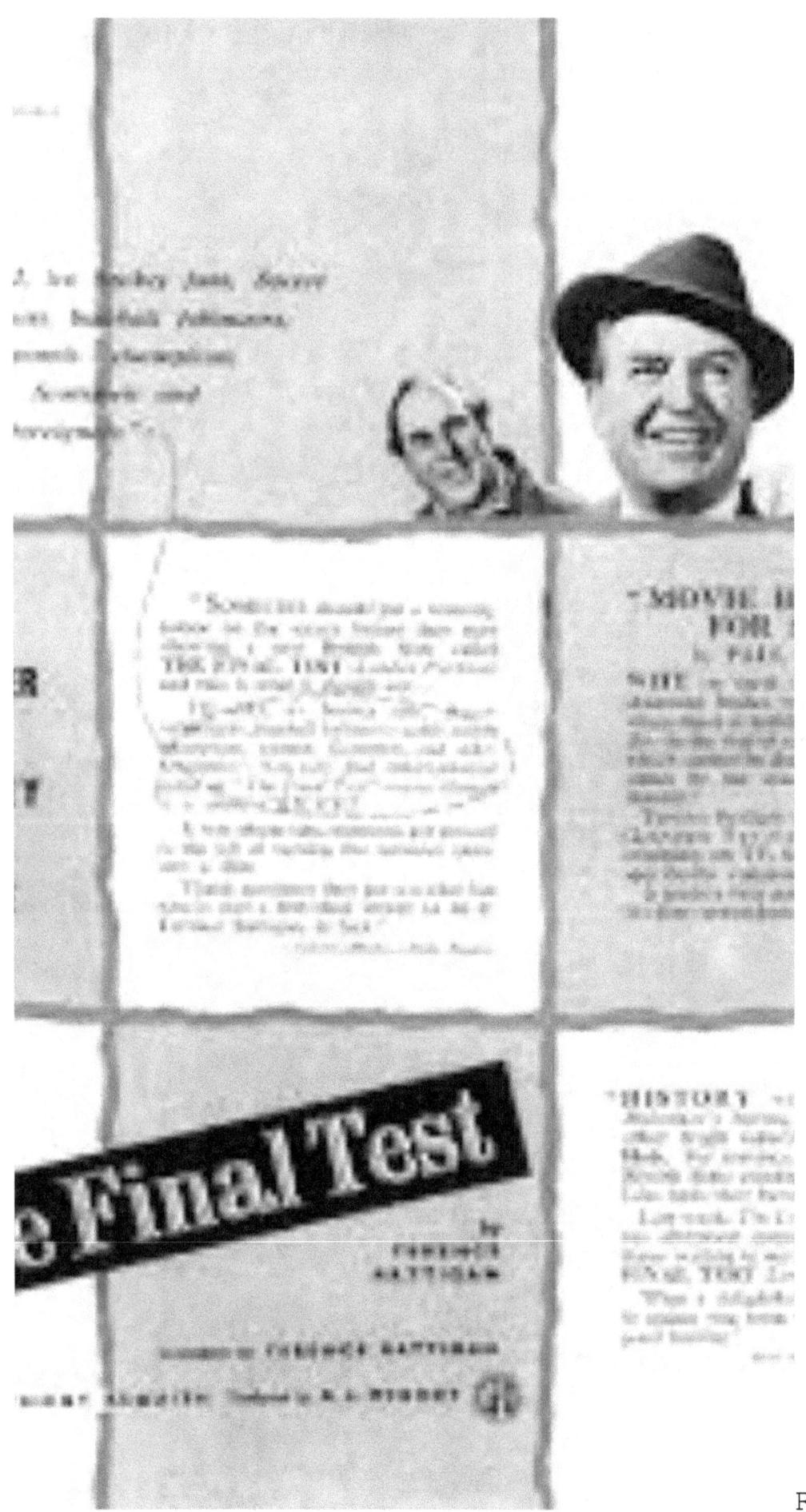

1953

Audio:

John Mortimer, Laurie Lee, 'Podmore, the <u>Spin</u>, Peter Tinniswood, <u>TMS</u>, <u>Wisden</u>…

**Cricket and Music**

In 1958 Cardus added Bruckner to his <u>Ten Composers</u> compiling a <u>Composers XI</u>

Super - Over /


( revised from Write Coach)

# International Cricket Culture

'the game appears to take on cultural valence unique
to its people'

- <u>American Sociological Review</u> / Harvard.edu 2005,
Vol 70

'[the next cricketer].. may come from Pudsey or
South Sydney, Nawanagar or Bridgetown but
wherever [he or she] comes from they will reshape
the medium to give new satisfactions to new
people.'

C L R James <u>Beyond a Boundary</u> 1963

'Some words and phrases used in cricket have
become idioms with a wider use [eg Not cricket]
the idiom is rather old-fashioned but still used
humorously'

<u>Oxford Guide to British and American Culture</u> 1999

'...a blinding light
an hour to play and the last man in..'

Newbolt / <u>Vitai Lampada</u> 1892

From Europe—

/w, E & N, S Yorkshire

/Leeds, Yorkshire

> London

 (Poem <u>MCMXIV</u> by P Larkin)

/Devon, Somerset

To Africa

# BLOOD, SWEAT AND TREASON

# HENRY OLONGA

# MY STORY

# Pitch

Sport
Racism
and
Resistan

**PETER HAIN**
**ANDRÉ ODENDAAL**

# Battles

# To the Americas

To Asia

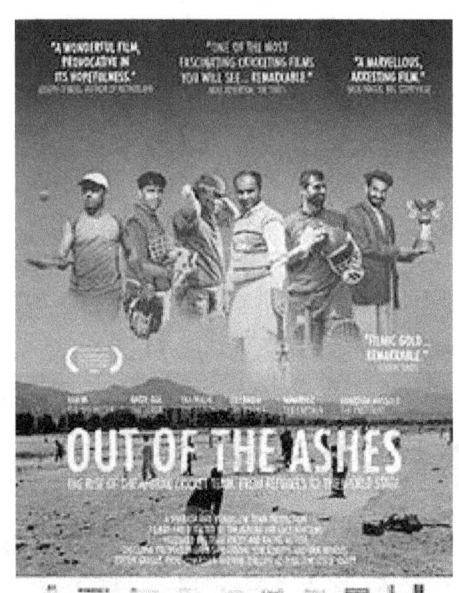

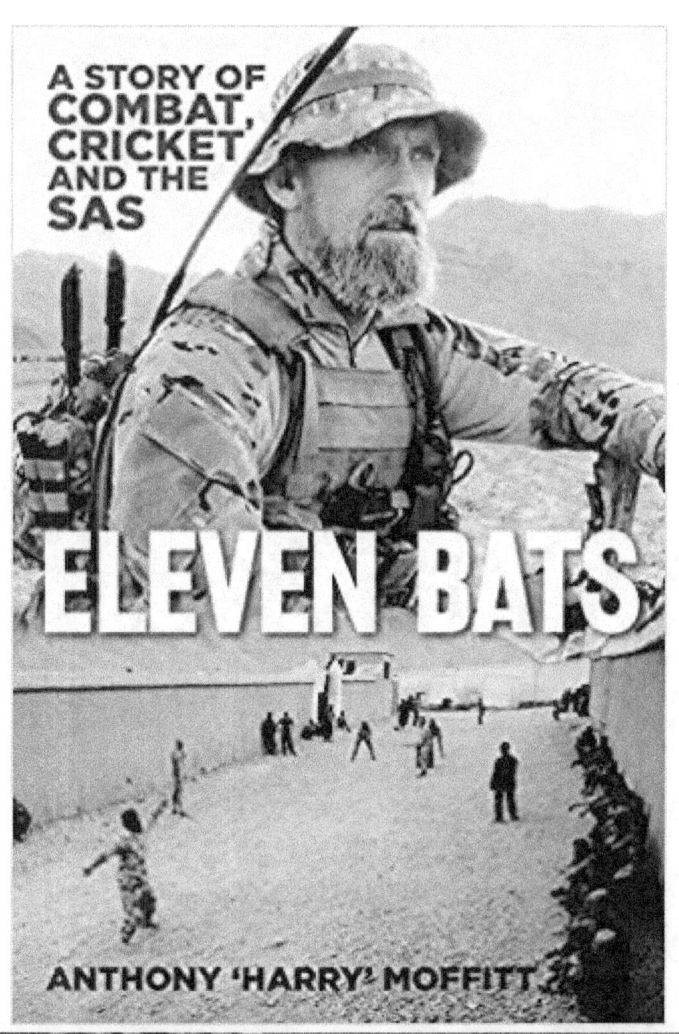

A STORY OF
COMBAT,
CRICKET
AND THE
SAS

ELEVEN BATS

ANTHONY 'HARRY' MOFFITT

SUBODH MUKERJI

*Love Marriage*

CHOOSE
WHO
YOU
BECOME

**Selection Day**

ALL EPISODES
**28 DEC** | NETFLIX

# CULTURE, CRICKET, FILMS AND MORE...

How media, entertainment and sports provide the cultural glue for India-UAE relationship

SPORTS ENTERTAINMENT MEDIA

Australasia...

## To Antarctica

# And beyond>

Also by **John F King** at

# York Europe Publications:

**Wise Guy and other fables**,  2008

ISBN 978-0-955851902

    **Wise Guy,**  2012, is also available as an eBook at Smashwords ISBN 9781476351735

\***Drama King** *I*  2010

ISBN 978-0-955851919

**Funky / Guy and other micro-fiction**,  2012

ISBN 978-0-955851964

**Micro-Waves**,  2012

ISBN 978-0-955851933

**Vienna, Love,**  2014

ISBN 978-0-955851971

Write  Coach,  2014

ISBN 978-0-955851988

Write Coach **II** 2015

ISBN 978-0-9931306-1-8

**A and  E** 2014

ISBN 978-0-955851995

**Prog**    2015

ISBN 978-0-9931306-0-1


**What's Left**  2016

ISBN 978-0-993106-2-5

**Low – Rise** 2016

ISBN 978-0-9931306-3-2

**SW10** 2017

ISBN 978-09931306-4-9

**West End Story** 2018

ISBN 978-0-993106-5-6

**Nice People** 2018

ISBN 978-0-99331306-6-3

**Memories of the Future** 2019

ISBN 978-09931306-7-0

**4 x 4** 2020

ISBN 978-0-9931306-8-7

**Drama King II** 2021

ISBN 978-1-716354335

*JFKMedia*

/Father Time Wall @ MCC Lords, London NW8

www.johnkinginternational.co.uk

Super-Over

# *John King International*

Supports –

MCC hub Yorkshire

 LORD'S TAVERNERS
Giving young people a sporting chance

# THE PRIMARY CLUB

LASHINGS
World XI

Super - Over

/ISBN 978-1-8383426-09

Super - Over

/ISBN 978-1-8383426-09

www.ingramcontent.com/pod-product-compliance
Lightning Source LLC
Chambersburg PA
CBHW080942170626
46811CB00009B/3220